ANIMALS of the Dark

Dear Reader

Have you ever felt a heavy python winding itself around your body? I have. That's me in the image on this page! Here is how it happened: when I was writing this book, I needed to take images of snake handler, Sean McCarthy, working with students at a primary school.

IT WAS FASCINATING TO WATCH SEAN CAREFULLY WINDING THE PYTHON AROUND THE STUDENTS, ONE BY ONE.

My sincere thanks to the following people for their time, information, images and enthusiasm for this book:

Stacey and Sean McCarthy, Melbourne, Australia

Catherine Cavedon and her Year 6 students at Mossgiel Park Primary School, Melbourne, Australia

Garry Maguire, Springbrook Research Centre, Springbrook, Australia

Belinda Janke and Stuart Webber, Queensland, Australia

Afterwards, it was my turn! All I could think about was, "I'm glad this snake is not venomous!"

Another fascinating topic in the book is about bed bugs – they're often in the news because they can annoy hotel guests around the world. Find out more about these blood-sucking nocturnal insects on pages 20–23.

I hope you enjoy reading this book!

Sharon Parsons

Contents

ANIMALS of the Dark

1 Nocturnal, Diurnal and Crepuscular Animals

All animals belong to one of three categories, depending on their level of activity at certain times: at night, through the day and during twilight.

TWILIGHT

Twilight refers to the early morning or early evening when the Sun is below the horizon and it is not quite light or dark.

Nocturnal Animals

Nocturnal animals are usually less active or asleep during the day and become more active at night in search of food.

Nocturnal Animal ID

Nocturnal animals have physical characteristics and needs that require them to be more active at night. For many nocturnal animals, there is also less competition for food in their habitat at night. For smaller animals with more predators, there is a greater chance of survival when hunting for food at night.

Diurnal Animals

Diurnal animals are more active during the day and are less active or sleep at night.

Diurnal Animals Can Be Nocturnal

Some diurnal animals, such as seabirds and sea turtles, check on their eggs in breeding sites at night-time to avoid predators.

Ostriches are diurnal but on moonlit nights they are active.

Crepuscular Animals

Crepuscular animals are more active during twilight. Crepuscular animals include: platypuses, rodents, wombats, deer, rabbits and rattlesnakes. Crepuscular insects include moths, flies and mosquitoes.

Crepuscular Animals Reduce Risks

Scientists believe that crepuscular animals reduce their risk of meeting predators during twilight because most predators are not active at this time. In hot climates, twilight conditions also help desert and rainforest animals to preserve their energy and reduce their need for extra water.

2 Nocturnal Senses

Even though some nocturnal animals, like owls and lemurs, have large eyes, many have poor eyesight. Therefore, they need to use one or more of their other senses to help them navigate through their habitat. These senses include touch, **echolocation** (in the case of bats and dolphins) and smell.

echolocation: see the Glossary, page 32.

an owl's eyes face forward

Life Science

Owls' Eyes

*An owl's large eyes face forward, just like human eyes, to give them good **stereoscopic vision**. But they are long-sighted so they cannot clearly focus on objects up close.*

stereoscopic vision: see the Glossary, page 32.

NIGHT OWLS

People are referred to as "night owls" when they prefer staying up late into the night.

Animals' Eyes at Night

Most nocturnal animals are less active during the day and inhabit darker places to reduce the amount of light entering their highly sensitive-to-light eyes. At night, their pupils increase in size to enhance their night vision. A special part of their eyes called the "tapetum lucidum" assists them to see at night.

a lemur

The Tapetum Lucidum

The eye's tapetum lucidum reflects light back into the eye like a mirror. The tapetum lucidum improves the sight of nocturnal animals in low-light conditions. Refer to page 26 for the complete diagram of a shark's eye and its tapetum lucidum.

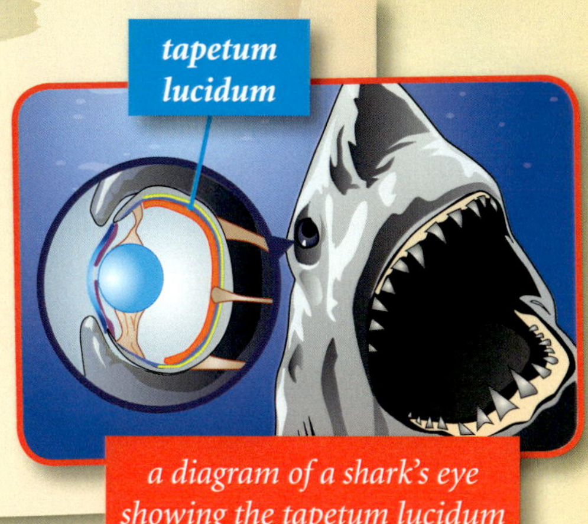

a diagram of a shark's eye showing the tapetum lucidum

Eyeshine

The eye's tapetum lucidum can also cause eyeshine that is visible to others when lights shine on animal eyes at night. Various colours of eyeshine include yellow, red, white and blue, depending on the animal species.

The helmet gecko's eyeshine is yellow.

a helmet gecko

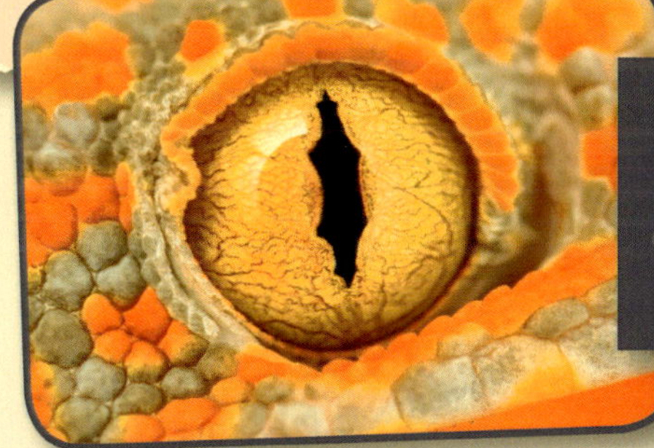

Scientists in Sweden have studied a nocturnal gecko, the helmet gecko, and found that the structure of its eyes enables it to see colours at night. Its eyes are about 350 times more powerful than those of humans.

Q: DO HUMANS HAVE A TAPETUM LUCIDUM IN THEIR EYES?

A: No. This causes photographs of some people to end up with the red-eye effect, as light shines straight onto the back of the eye.

a photograph showing the red-eye effect

3 Nocturnal Snakes

Snakes are cold-blooded reptiles, so they need the warmth of the Sun to create a enough body temperature to be active. However, many snakes do come out at night to hunt.

a species of milk snake

Two snakes that are nocturnal are the brown tree snake and the milk snake. The brown tree snake is found in Australia and Papua New Guinea, and some species of milk snake live in South America, the USA and Canada.

The red areas show where most of the brown tree snakes can be found.

a brown tree snake

Compare Two Nocturnal Snakes

	Milk Snake	Brown Tree Snake
Habitat	Forests, valleys, mountains, near wetlands, outbuildings	Rainforest trees, rock crevices, caves, roof cavities
Size	Adults grow up to about 150 cm	Adults grow up to about 150 cm
Toxicity	Non-venomous	Can be venomous for children
Behaviour	Appear nervous and can become aggressive if startled	Very aggressive
Food	Small rodents, birds, frogs, lizards and other snakes	Birds, bird eggs, bats, frogs, small mammals and lizards
Common Misconceptions	They drink milk (no, they don't)	They always live in trees (no, they don't)
Pupil Shape	Eyes have round pupils	Eyes have vertical slit pupils

Diurnal Snake Eyes

Diurnal snakes usually have round-shaped pupils, like most diurnal creatures.

a diurnal snake's round-shaped pupils

Nocturnal Snake Eyes

Nocturnal snakes usually have vertical slit pupils that they can easily enlarge to absorb more light during the night.

a nocturnal snake's vertical slit pupils

A Snake Handler in School

Sean McCarthy is a snake handler. He enjoys visiting schools around Victoria, Australia, to educate students about snakes and safety. But he doesn't take venomous snakes to the schools!

Sean came up with the idea to visit schools because his family has always been passionate about reptiles and kept many as pets.

Many students are surprised to find that a snake's skin is dry, not slimy.

Life Science

A Snake for a Pet

The corn snake, also known as the red rat snake, can be found in parts of the USA. It makes a good pet because it has a calm nature and is easy to look after. It grows to about one metre in length and has an attractive, colourful pattern. People can keep snakes in a serpentarium – a special place for snakes to live safely.

Sean introducing students to a new "classmate"

"This is the heaviest necklace I've ever had around my neck!"

"I think I prefer carrying my backpack!"

"I just have to keep calm and still."

"Well, that's a handful!"

4 Nocturnal Action Inside Caves

Filming **Inside** Dark **Elephant** Caves

Kenya

Night has fallen in the Kitum Caves in Mt Elgon National Park in Kenya, Africa. A television crew has set up special infra-red lights that can't be detected by animals but will enable them to be filmed. The TV crew hear the sound of animals walking slowly up a steep pitch-black path. But not all the animals can fit through the cave entrance so many have to turn away.

Mt Elgon National Park

elephants on their way to the Kitum Caves at night

Kitum Caves

Salt-Hungry Elephants

The cameras capture salt-hungry elephants rumbling into the dark caves. With their strong tusks, they scrape and break salt-rich rocks from the cave walls to extract as much salt as possible. Other animals such as bushbuck, hyena and buffalo lick the salty rocks that fall to the ground.

a hyena carries her cub

Hyenas

Inside the dark cave, animals such as the bushbuck need to be careful if a predator like the hyena is there for dinner, too!

Kitum Cave Walls

Parts of the caves have weakened and collapsed because the elephants have mined the walls for salty rocks over many years.

salt-hungry elephants inside the Kitum Caves

Wetas

A weta is a large insect, similar in appearance to a grasshopper or a cricket. All wetas are nocturnal and they only live in New Zealand. They have been called the dinosaur of the insect world because they have been around since the time of the dinosaurs! There are over 70 species of weta, and some are among the largest and heaviest insects in the world.

NEW ZEALAND

Tusked Weta in Battle

A tusked male weta "dressed" in armour, with long, raised back legs, terrifying tusks and waving antennae can look scary. Its appearance and behaviour is a natural defence against other male weta, especially when they butt each other in battle. But weta are harmless to humans, unless they feel threatened.

Life Science

Predators of Weta

Native predators of the weta in New Zealand are the tuatara, the saddleback (bird) and the laughing owl.

a tusked weta

Cave Wetas

Cave wetas are flightless, and during the day they actively move around in caves and hide in damp, dark places, such as under logs. At night, many cave weta search the forest floor for vegetation and dead insects.

a cave weta

Weta Sounds

Most species of weta have ears and make sounds at night-time, but cave weta have no ears and make no sounds. The cave weta's long antennae are about four times the length of its body, which helps it to find its way around in the dark.

a male tree weta

a female tree weta

5 Why Do Glow-Worms Glow?

Nocturnal **Larvae**

If you are lucky enough to be in the right place as night falls, you may witness clusters of glow-worms that look like fairy lights. The right kinds of places include dark cave walls and ceilings, steep earth walls along roads and around rock ledges.

But what are glow-worms and how do they glow?

Glow-worms are not actually glowing worms. They are a type of insect (either a fly or a beetle, depending on the species) that glows at different stages of their life cycle, through what is known as "bioluminescence".

Bioluminescent Larvae

In Australia and New Zealand, the native glow-worms are the bioluminescent larvae of flies that look like mosquitoes. Larvae are also known as maggots.

The Glow

The tip of the larva's tail emits a tiny blue–green glow, which is why you only see tiny dots of light. The tail tip is the larva's excretory tube, and this is where a chemical reaction occurs to create the glow.

a glow-worm

Stuart Webber is a specialist photographer of glow-worms. His images are above and belo

Equation Chart to Describe the Chemical Reaction for a Glow-Worm's Glow

Larva waste
+ an enzyme
+ an energy molecule
+ oxygen

= the glow

The ability to glow is a natural phenomenon that takes place for nine months in the glow-worm's life cycle.

Why Glow-Worms Glow

It appears that different types of larvae glow for various reasons. It is believed that one type of larva glows to warn predators against eating them, as they are mildly toxic. Another type of larva seems to glow to attract prey, such as midges, to eat.

Some larvae do not emit a bright enough light on full-Moon nights. They are glowing, but not as brightly as more mature larvae. Glow-worms also have a clever ability to stop glowing if they sense danger in their webs. They stop the glow by shutting down the bioluminescent chemical reaction in their tail's excretory tube.

More to Learn

Not much is known about glow-worms, as their nocturnal habits and generally remote environments make it difficult to collect information. However, scientists are continuing to add to the existing body of knowledge. Glow-worms are a unique insect. Their tiny lights remind us to look after their natural environment, so they continue to be seen in the future.

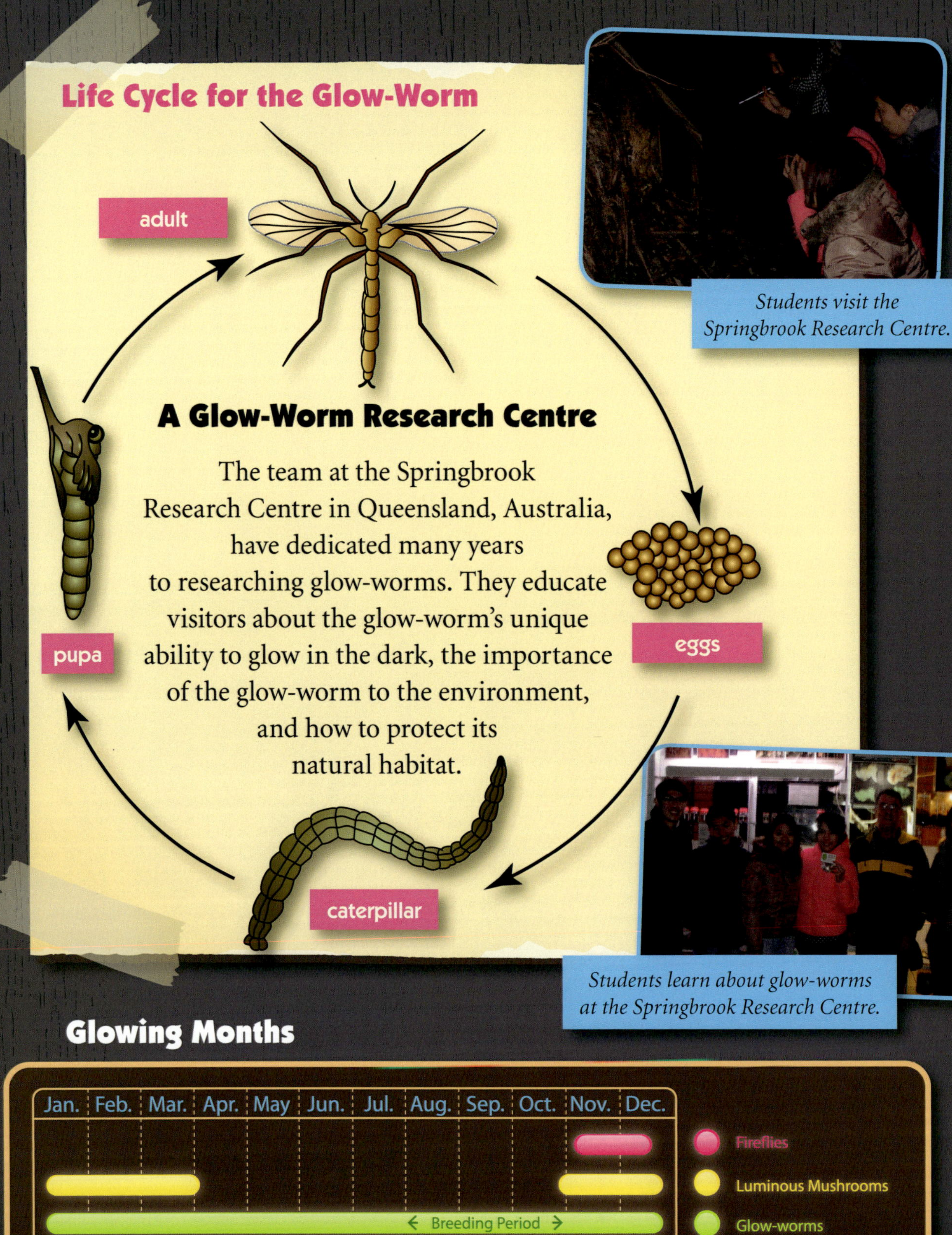

A Glow-Worm Research Centre

The team at the Springbrook Research Centre in Queensland, Australia, have dedicated many years to researching glow-worms. They educate visitors about the glow-worm's unique ability to glow in the dark, the importance of the glow-worm to the environment, and how to protect its natural habitat.

Students visit the Springbrook Research Centre.

Students learn about glow-worms at the Springbrook Research Centre.

Glowing Months

Unlike fireflies or luminous mushrooms, glow-worms display bioluminescence throughout the year.

glow-worms in the Waitomo Caves

Glow-Worms at the Waitomo Caves

On New Zealand's North Island, many people enjoy visiting the famous Waitomo Caves to see thousands of glow-worms.

The subterranean caverns were first opened for tourists in 1889 by the local Māori chief, Tane Tinorau, and his wife, Huti.

From 1906, the New Zealand Government looked after the caves, but by 1989 the caves' administration was returned to the local Māori tribe. Today, some of staff at the Waitomo Caves are direct descendants of Tane Tinorau and Huti.

Q: WHERE DID GLOW-WORMS GET THEIR NAME?

A: It is thought that when early British settlers arrived in Australia and New Zealand, they named the glowing larvae "glow-worms". In England, glow-worms are glowing beetles that are shaped like worms.

glow-worms on a rock face

6 Blood-Sucking Bed Bugs

The **Dracula** of Insects

Bed Bugs

Although not scientifically classified as a nocturnal insect, bed bugs are more active at night. These parasites climb silently into millions of beds around the world towards unsuspecting humans to suck their blood. They like any warm bed, whether it is clean or not.

Watch out for bed bugs that look like brownish-red, wingless insects – they want your blood!

Bed Bug Species

There are two main species of bed bugs: tropical bed bugs (they prefer warmer climates) and common bed bugs (they prefer cooler climates).

bed bugs at work

Life Cycle for the Bed Bug

Eggs: Ten Days

After mating, the female lays about three sticky white eggs a day. The eggs adhere to rough surfaces in a range of hiding places and, in warmer climates, they will hatch in ten days. But in colder climates, the eggs can take a few weeks to hatch.

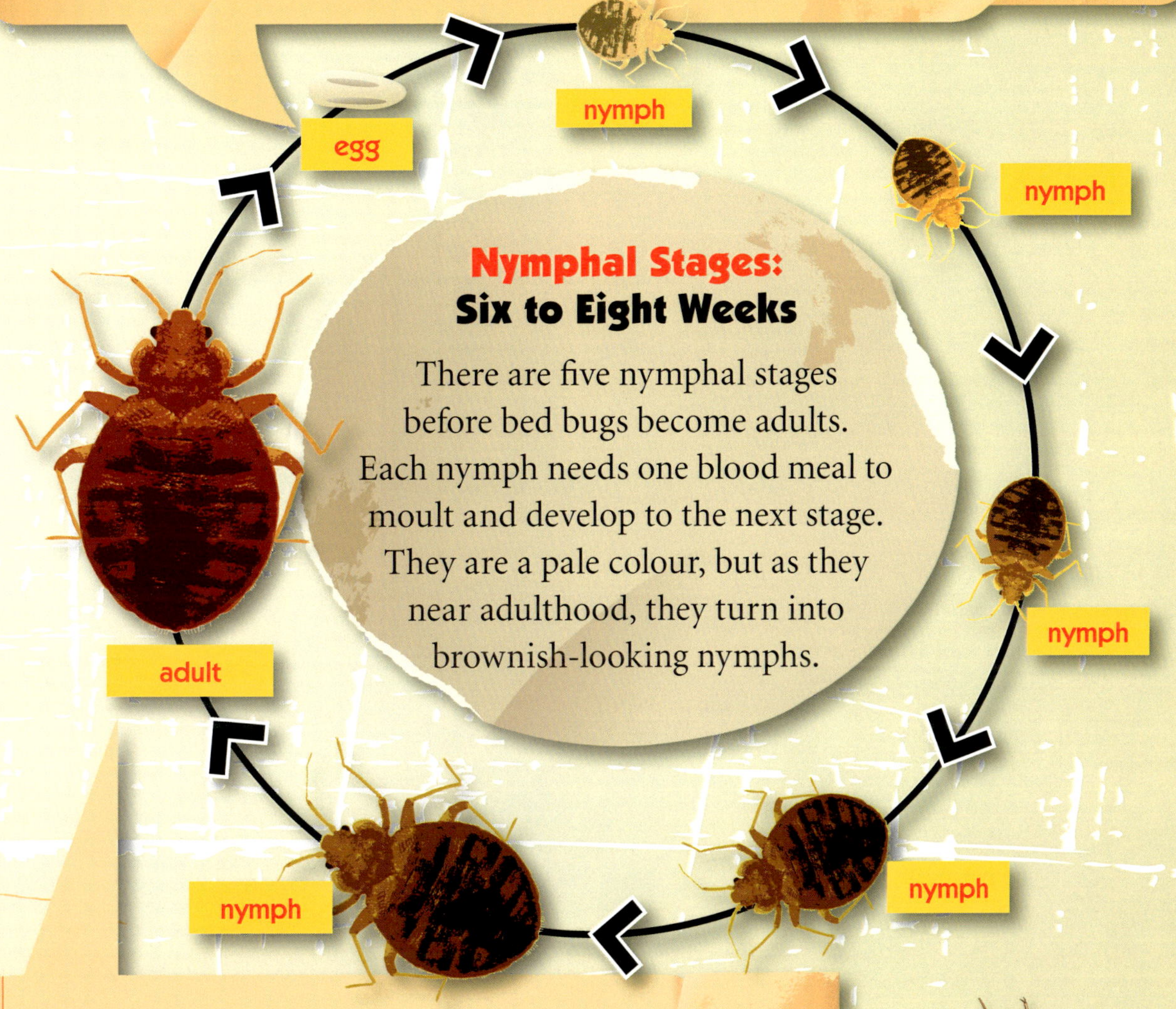

Nymphal Stages: Six to Eight Weeks

There are five nymphal stages before bed bugs become adults. Each nymph needs one blood meal to moult and develop to the next stage. They are a pale colour, but as they near adulthood, they turn into brownish-looking nymphs.

Adult Stage: Six Months

Adult bed bugs can live for up to six months in warm conditions, and longer in colder climates. They need blood for continued development and nutrition. They swell in size after a meal of blood!

Bed Bug Questions Answered

Q Do bed bugs bite other warm-blooded animals?

A Yes, but only if they're desperate for some blood. They prefer humans!

Q Why do they hide under beds?

A They hide in lots of dark places, many of which are close to where people sleep. But they can only detect a food source that's five to ten centimetres away.

Q What does a bed bug inject into a person?

A A bed bug injects a fluid to help it obtain the blood. It is this fluid that causes a person's skin to itch, redden and swell.

Q Do they need blood every day?

A No, they can survive for weeks without "food", depending on how warm it is.

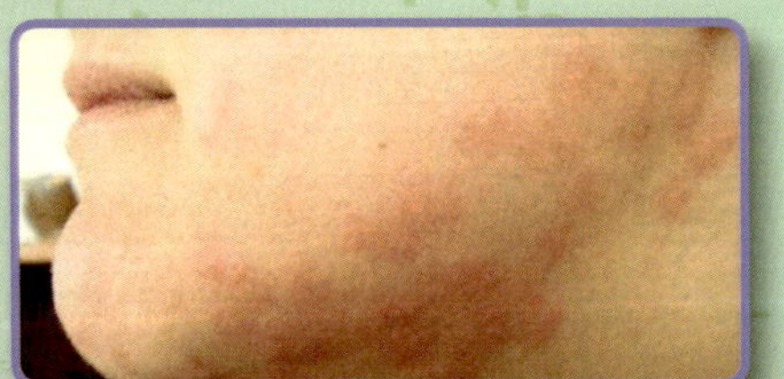

Q What happens when bed bugs become engorged with blood?

A When they are full with blood they increase in size and their colour changes from brown to red.

Q Do bed bugs smell?

A Yes, their scent glands emit an odour.

Q Why is there an outbreak of bed bugs around the world?

A They are great travellers. They are transported from place to place in suitcases and freight.

> "BED BUGS CAN TRAVEL BETWEEN HOTEL ROOMS THROUGH POWER POINTS."

KISSING BUGS

Kissing bugs are nocturnal parasites that usually bite uncovered facial areas of sleeping people.

a bed bug biting

a swollen area from bed bug bites

Life Science

Blood-Sucking Insects

As well as bed bugs, there are other blood-sucking insects, such as fleas, mosquitoes, ticks and lice. These insects are called parasites because they need a host (a human or another animal) for their food.

a tick

a flea

How to Check for Bed Bugs

When you first enter a hotel room or a new place, this is how to check if bed bugs are present:

1. pull the bed away from the wall
2. check the top of the mattress for tiny blood spots
3. check below the mattress for small brownish-red insects.

What to Do if You're Bitten

Everyone's bodies react in different ways, but most people end up with lines of red, itchy welts after a bed bug bite. Try not to scratch as it can worsen the condition.

Make sure you wash the area. Ask an adult to apply a lotion to reduce the redness and itchiness.

7 Nocturnal Marine Life

Many species of marine fish are classified as nocturnal and, in deep, dark waters, they use the senses of touch and sound (including echolocation) to help them find food and evade predators.

Who turned out the lights?

Features of Nocturnal Fish

Nocturnal fish:

- may not swim as fast as diurnal fish
- generally have larger eyes
- can be solitary rather than living in schools (which exposes them more to predators)
- demonstrate shy behaviour by hiding in places like caves
- can be colours that are not easily seen underwater, such as red or yellow/brown
- tend to be carnivores (diurnals are usually herbivores or omnivores)
- may be able to sense water movement to locate prey.

Recognise these **Nocturnal** Marine Animals?

Fish

Nocturnal fish include snapper, eels, flashlight fish and scorpion fish.

snapper

eel

flashlight fish

scorpion fish

Coral Polyps

Coral live at shallow depths on coral reefs because they need light to survive.

At night, coral polyps come out of their skeletons and use their long, stinging tentacles to feed on floating zooplankton, or tiny fish.

coral polyp

Crustaceans

Nocturnal crustaceans include shrimp, crabs and starfish.

shrimp

crab

starfish

Finding Food in the **Dark**

A Shark's Vision

In the low-visibility waters of the ocean, a shark can see very well because it has eyes on either side of its head, giving it an almost 360-degree field of vision. It also has a tapetum lucidum layer of tissue in each eye – like most nocturnal animals. (See pages 6–7 for more information about the tapetum lucidum.)

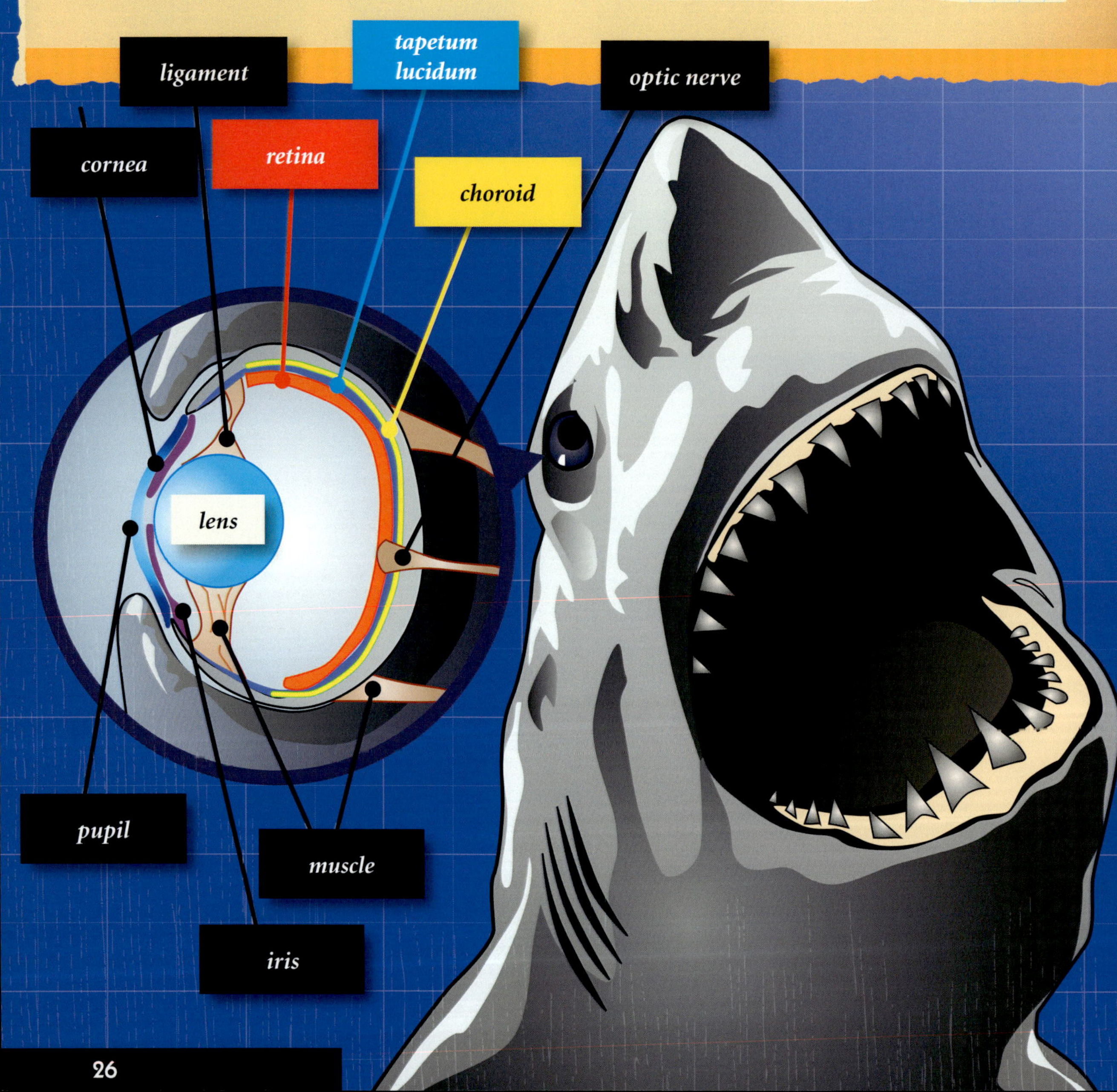

Dolphins and Echolocation

Dolphins are not naturally nocturnal but they can be when food is scarce. They use the sense of echolocation to locate food.

a seal on the hunt

A Seal's Sense of Smell

Seals can swim to deep, dark areas of the ocean in search of food. They need a lot of food, so they spend many hours each day exploring the oceans. Seals can see very well but in dark waters they find their prey by relying on their whiskers and their sense of smell. Their whiskers are very sensitive to vibration and movement in the water.

Young seals grow quickly and learn how to swim and hunt from a very early age – some species can hunt from as young as three to six weeks of age.

8 Nocturnal Pollination of Plants

Nocturnal plants rely on certain insects to pollinate them at twilight and at night. Some plants open their flowers at night to invite pollination. For example, the Madonna lily and a night-blooming jasmine rely on moths for pollination.

This Madonna lily uses its large white, open-shaped flowers to attract moths at night for pollination.

a night-blooming jasmine

The hawk moth is a nocturnal species that pollinates flowers.

Stop Nectar Thieves

Many night-pollinated flowers close during the day to prevent day-time pollinators from taking their nectar and pollen. Conversely, many daytime-pollinated flowers close at night for the same reason.

Nectar Needed for Migration

When pollinators such as birds, bats and butterflies migrate, they need nectar "meals" for the long journeys. As more forests and gardens are destroyed for building developments, fewer nectar-producing plants are available.

How We Can Help

To encourage natural pollination humans can:

- reduce or stop using pesticides on plants
- plant more native, nectar-producing plants
- leave tree stumps for nesting sites.

Bats, the Night-Time Pollinators

Typical day-time pollinators include birds and bees, but at night-time many species of bat come out to pollinate certain flowers and fruit trees.

Bats pollinate fruit including bananas, mangos and guavas. It is estimated that bats pollinate over 500 different types of tropical plants every year.

At night, bats use echolocation to locate and pollinate flowers that are not brightly coloured and don't give off strong scents. On the other hand, birds and bees are attracted to flowers with bright colours and strong scents. It's a good example of nature working in harmony.

A bee pollinates a plant.

Life Science

Bats Beat the Pests

Bats are natural pest controllers. They eat insects that are harmful for bugs. This minimises the need for artificial pesticides.

A bat is out for a night-time hunt.

9 Nocturnal Kiwi at Risk

Drought **Affects** the Kiwi

Sometimes environmental factors affect the behaviour of nocturnal animals. In New Zealand, the kiwi is a flightless bird whose nocturnal activity protects it from predators.

However, during the 2009–2010 drought in Northland, on the North Island of New Zealand, food and water became so scarce that many kiwis had to resort to finding food and water during the day.

The flightless kiwi forages for food.

Index

Glossary

bioluminescence The production of light by a living organism, where energy is released by a chemical reaction in the organism's body

bushbuck A type of antelope found in Africa. It can be dangerous and has sharp horns.

echolocation The method of locating objects using the time i takes for an echo to return and the direction it returns from. Many animals use echolocation.

pollination The process by which plants are fertilised with pollen

stereoscopic vision When the same object is viewed with both eyes at the same time, therefore allowing for depth and distance perception.

subterranean Existing below the surface of the Earth

weta A large nocturnal insect found in New Zealand The name "weta" comes from the Māori language.

zooplankton Tiny organisms found in oceans, seas and fresh water